Green Witch

Green Witch

Scholastic Press · New York

ALICE HOFFMAN

Library of Congress Cataloging-in-Publication Data · Hoffman, Alice · Green witch / Alice Hoffman. — 1st ed. · p. cm. · Summary: A year after her world was nearly destroyed, sixteen-year-old Green has become the one villagers turn to for aid, especially to record their stories, but Green will need the help of other women who, like herself, are believed to be witches if she is to find her best friend and her one true love.

ISBN 978-0-545-14195-6 · [1. Storytelling—Fiction. 2. Missing persons—Fiction. 3. Grief—Fiction. 4. Supernatural—Fiction. 5. Gardening—Fiction. 6. Orphans—Fiction.] I. Title. · PZ7.H67445Grg 2010 · [Fic]—dc22 · 2009017606 · 10 9 8 7 6 5 4 3   10 11 12 13 14 · The text type was set in Adobe Garamond. · Book design by Elizabeth B. Parisi · Printed in the U.S.A.   23 First edition, March 2010

Green Witch

This is what I remembered

What you dream, you can grow.

Someone told me that, but I didn't believe it.

    I said I had nothing and that people with nothing are unable to dream. But I was wrong. Dreams are like air. They never leave you. It takes less than nothing to begin. Start with a pile of rocks. Moonstones, night stones, stones the color of snow. Start with heartache, thorns, vines. Let there be mud on your clothes, nails in your boots, ink on your skin, pain deep inside you. Let it grow and don't be afraid.

Start with your own story.

I lost everything — my mother, my father, my sister, Aurora. They went into the city on the day of the disaster. My last words to them were not pretty. I wanted to be the one to cross the river. I was hurt and resentful. I wanted more. But I was the one who stayed home to work in the garden. It was my sister's turn to visit the city that I loved so much, not mine.

I wasn't with them when they died.

Afterward, I didn't want to move forward from that moment when our world fell apart. My garden was chalk and ashes after the city across the river burned down. Cinders covered the countryside. But time changes things, like it or not. Now, a year later, whatever I plant grows overnight. I can hear my garden in my dreams, unfolding, flourishing. Each morning I have to take an ax and cut back the vines or my cottage will disappear into the thicket.

Every one of my roses is blood red. Red to remind me of all that is gone — my family, my city, the life I led before. Blood red to remind me that despite everything, I'm alive. I'm still bleeding.

A few survivors managed to escape. They set out on rafts even though the river itself was on fire, every wave roiling with embers. Those who made it to our shores told us that the people who destroyed the city call themselves the Horde. They had been coming down from the mountains in secret for years, setting up shops, befriending their neighbors in the city, biding their time.

Once the city had been destroyed, they announced that their mission was to put an end to everything we had built. They said we had only ourselves to blame for what happened — the sheets of flame, the skies of death. They believed it wasn't their fires that had destroyed us, but what we had built — our trains and libraries and bridges, even our schools — that had brought us to ruin. They want to go back to a time when men toiled in the fields without plows and trucks, when women were shut into their houses, sweeping, cooking, never daring to speak back.

They insist the fire that killed so many was an act of heaven meant to punish us for our sins. *Repent*, they tell us. *Join with us. Don't even try to fight, because heaven is on our side. Angels ride on the backs of our black horses.*

But my sister, Aurora, was there in the city that day, selling vegetables from our truck, and I know she hadn't sinned. She was a globe of light, a white dove. Heaven would have never burned her alive.

Only a year ago, the world seemed dead. We hid in our houses. We cursed our fate. Some of us used our regret and grief to destroy ourselves. Everywhere you went, people were in shock, wondering why they had survived when so many had not.

I know. Twelve months have passed, but often it's the only thing I can see, even when I close my eyes. I was on the hillside when my family set up our vegetable stand in our favorite market-place. I saw the spark, the flames, the red walls that trapped everyone I loved.

That day I stood on our side of the river and had no choice but to look. I looked until I couldn't see anything anymore.

I watched as my world disappeared.

Now there are buds on the trees. There are fish in the river — silver eels, trout with blue scales. The Horde keeps a watchful eye on us, but they have allowed the bridge to the city to be rebuilt, made of logs and rope and hard work. Our village has begun to trade with the few survivors who remain in the city. Some of those who were there when the explosions happened are burned. Some are mute and some are so easily startled they dart away whenever they see birds in the sky. They live underground, equally frightened by the light and the darkness. They no longer trust strangers. They appear in the marketplace when they are desperate. They offer those who come to trade with them gold and diamonds in exchange for barrels of clean water, blankets, clothes for their children. Nothing works in the city. There are no church bells, no trains, no radios, no schools, no stores. Still, whenever they're asked if they want to leave, the few who remain always refuse.

We'll rebuild, they say. *It will just take time.*

In our village, life has moved forward. We once relied on the city for nearly everything, including our clothes, our building materials, our water. Now a well stands in the center of the town square, and the water we draw in wooden buckets is clean and cold. An old man who was a professor at the university in the city has taught some local boys how to build the windmills that dot the fields. It has been difficult piecing back together all we once had. We are lucky to have the Finder, a mysterious person who lives in the woods. This curious individual leaves out parts of machines that are useful. If you need it, he can find whatever you desire among the ruins of villages that have been deserted. No one has seen the Finder, but there are many strange people in the countryside now.

The world has changed, so it only makes sense that people have changed as well. There are women who live in trees, men who sit on rooftops keeping watch for looters, bands of orphans who refused to come back to town until the woman who had been our teacher gathered them up like wildflowers. There's Uncle Tim, who is nobody's uncle but seems kindly enough and has been adopted by the village. He washed up onshore after the fires and now cares for abandoned dogs at his campsite in the woods.

These are the people who can't get past that

terrible day. We know them, and leave them to their grief. We avoid the woman who sits at the banks of the river and howls when the moon is full. We never bother the man who lost his beloved and has torn out all his hair. Loss does different things to different people. Some fall apart. Some, like the Finder, rebuild. I have done both. I have crawled under my table and refused to come out. I have covered myself with thorns and tattoos. I have planted a garden, reached out to my neighbors, begun to write down my story.

Surely, I can never sit in judgment of the lost or the found.

If you want something from the Finder, it's easy enough. Write a note and leave it in the notch of the big elm tree at the fork in the road. Leave a gift alongside. Not money — we don't use that anymore. Something useful — a set of measuring spoons or a can of soup, a hammer or an apple pie. Whatever you're looking for will be there within the week. It may be battered, it may be in pieces, but still, it will arrive. The Finder has managed to avoid the Horde's spies by limiting his movements to the cover of darkness. Because of his efforts, there are now generators that are run by hand. Lights flicker in the darkness. There are iceboxes, stoves, medicine kits. Because of him, a bell has been found to sit atop town hall. It rings twice a day, at dawn and at dusk, reminding us there are still hours in the day.

I had always been a city girl at heart. Moving there had been my dream. That was no longer true. The city I'd loved was in ruins. I thought of it as a graveyard, the past, not the future.

On the day of the bridge reopening, when a big festival was held, I couldn't go any farther than the tollgate. I stood there with my sister's little dog, Onion, beside me. I couldn't take another step.

There were jugglers on the bridge and Uncle

Tim played the guitar. The schoolteacher had the children make banners.

I walked away.

I wasn't ready to see the place where my family had perished. I couldn't go back to the city I had always loved. I have heard there are no longer bodies in the streets or blood on the cobblestones, but my beloved city is still in pieces, the buildings like silver stars — some fallen, some rising, some constant in the sky.

I live alone in my cottage, deep in the woods. I rarely go into the village. I'm too busy working in my garden. I wear simple clothes: a green shirt, a faded skirt, green suede boots or bare feet. I tie up my long black hair with string. People in the village are polite. But they stare at me because of my tattoos even though I am their neighbor and they all know my name. Green, who can be depended on. Green, who has walked through to the other side of sorrow.

Sometimes when they stare I wonder if they can see something I can't.

All through the winter, people came to me when they were hungry. They begged at my fence. Neighbors I had known in another lifetime, people who had always ignored me — the sheriff, the mayor, the shopkeeper's wife who had tried to cheat me in exchange for my mother's candlesticks and jewelry — all asked for my help. I have become someone they turn to. I can tell the false from the real, the truth from a lie, just as I am certain that when the leaves of a plum tree curl inward there are beetles at work in the bark. I know that when I reach my hands into the soil, my garden will heal and grow.

I had been Green, too shy to speak to strangers. Green, who kept her inner self hidden away. I am someone different now. They come to me not just for apples and lettuce, but for advice, remedies, solace. I try to be of help. I remember my mother's kindness, my father's strength, my sister's delight in the beauty of the world. I think of what they might have said or done.

Women stand by my fence and cry over lost love until I offer them packets of mint tea to help them sleep at night. Children beg for sweets knowing I'll give them strawberries and honey, or slices of rhubarb pie. The town councilmen ask me when the corn should be planted and where the new well should be dug.

I stand in the meadow until the sun strikes me at noon and say, *Plant here.*

I point to the place where the swamp cabbages grow, a marshy spot, the mark of an underground spring. *Here,* I tell them. *Dig your well.*

There is something else I'm known for. Another reason they come to me.

I tell their stories.

When embers whirled across the river, books were the first thing to burn. The school turned to ash. Our library has no roof. The few editions that remain are mostly unreadable. The print has dripped off the pages, pooling into inky rivers on the floorboards. Mice live in the stacks, eating the bookbinding glue, tearing up what remains of atlases and encyclopedias for their nests. Any volumes that were left were used as fuel, tossed into fireplaces and stoves during that first harsh winter.

I began by writing on myself, ink and pins on my own skin. I covered myself with tattoos, but when I was done, I still had more stories to tell. I started to write on clean white pages, the last of the paper that was left. I wrote about my family going to the city to sell vegetables, about my school friend Heather, who had lived in the woods, then disappeared, and about a boy I had never expected to walk past the garden gate, into my life. I wrote about who I was and who I would become and who I wanted to be.

When I ran out of ink, I made my own from

the sap of the black lilies that grow in the far-thest fields. It's an extract from the flower's heart; it won't wash away or smear.

Because they know I'm a writer, people in the village come to me. Even those who rarely speak, who seem closed off, who prefer to run away and hide rather than converse, arrive at my door. Some wear shawls over their heads as they come up the steps. They don't want to be seen. Each has a different story, but they all pose a single question once their stories have been told. Why did they live when so many others did not? Why have they lost all they treasured most in this world?

One after the other they sit at my kitchen table, where my mother once shelled peas, where my father drank his coffee, rich with sugar and cream, where my sister painted watercolors of our family, our garden, our life. It's here that the townspeople tell me the stories of their lives. The mistakes they made, the people they loved, the way it all used to be before the world as we knew it disappeared.

There are other people who trail after me when I come to town, desperate to talk, holding tight to my sleeve. These people have so much to say, a single volume isn't enough. They're the ones who know that our stories are all we have now.

Before long, I had written down so many stories I ran out of paper. I began to make my own. I used chopped-up rags and celery stalks, boiled oak leaves, water, ground chestnut flour. Maybe that's why some people whisper about me, even the ones who depend on me for their vegetables and fruit, who wouldn't have made it through the winter without me. They've seen the kettle I keep in the yard, set over a stack of burning wood. They've seen the plumes of black smoke rise.

When the mixture in the cauldron has turned soupy, I push it through a screen from an old window and let it dry in sheets set out in the sun until they harden. Then I cut the sheets with a pair of gardening shears.

At last, there it is.

I am the first to make paper again. If anything is magic, this is. I dream of paper as if it were a garden, sheaves of white and green, fields of it, reams of it, all smelling like spring. I never realized how beautiful paper was before. I took it for granted. I didn't rub it between my fingers or hold it up to the light.

I add different elements depending on the person whose story needs telling. Certain ingredients are right for certain stories. When someone asks how I know what to add to the mix, I ask, *How do you know the difference between the sun and the moon?* The answer is obvious, at least to me.

For the old man who knows about windmills, I added grass to the paper. You might think a man who'd once been a scientist at a university would want a clean white page, but he told me how windmills could create energy, run water pumps, turn everything green.

For the baker, who had lost his only son in the city on the terrible firestorm day, I added cloves and the last of the cinnamon from a metal container in my mother's baking cupboard. He held the paper up to his nose and breathed deeply, then wept. His story was a true baker's book — recipes for strudel and pecan pie and Sacher tortes, things we didn't have the ingredients for anymore, mythical cakes and pies that made my mouth water.

For the woman who had been my teacher, who had lost all of her books, I added a stray page I had found from her favorite novel. The paper turned a dovelike gray and smelled like heather and heath. The story my teacher dictated to me was a list of all of the novels she had loved, along with a description of exactly where she'd been when she'd read each one. She had been sprawled in a chair in the parlor of her grandmother's house right in the center of the city on a hot summer day when she'd read her favorite book of all. Because of that, and because of the incendiary nature of the love affair in the novel, the paper her story was written on was always hot to the touch.

For Uncle Tim, who was a survivor, I added ashes from that day. I had saved them in a glass bottle. When I poured in the ashes, it was like adding a storm to the mix. Uncle Tim was a hermit now because he no longer trusted men, only the stray dogs he adopted. He had seen terrible things on that day — people on fire, people leaping from ledges. He had tried to rescue several of his neighbors, but none had survived. He wept when he told his story, so I added salt. The resulting paper was black with white edges. When you ran your hand across it, tears came to your eyes.

You could hear a faraway voice say *Save me* even when no one else was in the room.

I felt it was my duty to collect these stories just as surely as if they had grown in my garden on stalks and stems, as if they had ripened in the sun and were ready to pick, one by one.

This was the way I lived now. This was the way my garden grew.

I am Green, the one to turn to, the one to whom you can tell your story. I live alone, but the villagers accept me. They need me, and because of their need, they trust me as well.

Or so I had thought.

Lately, there has been talk of witches in our midst, women they call the Enchanted. People have suspicious minds, especially in difficult times. There are those who insist my garden is the only one that flourishes because of the potions I make. They say I can mix up a remedy or a curse depending on my mood. They whisper about my tattoos. The wings of the inked bats move, people vow. The vines grow. The roses have a scent stronger than perfume.

There are those who say if I have the talents of a witch, I must be dangerous. I go out of my way to say hello to these people. I even shake their hands. Whether someone thinks I am a farmer or a sorceress makes no difference. If they believe that writing a book is casting a spell, so be it.

If this is magic, then call me a witch.

No one knows the deepest truth. How can they? I hide it well.

Even though I have never used red ink, there is half of a red heart tattooed beneath my shirt. I've been in love. That is my deepest secret. The one I'll never tell. It's no one's business but my own. His name was Diamond and he left me.

He was nearly destroyed by the fire, his face half burned, his voice lost. He was the stranger who appeared in my garden when I expected my life to be empty. He was nothing to me, and then he was everything. I helped him to heal even though I knew that meant he would go off to search for his family. I thought he would come back. I thought we were meant to be together. But I haven't even received a letter. I know letters are difficult to send in our world—still, I thought he would have managed somehow.

Being alone for so long, I've grown bitter. Every night I waited for him, and every night he disappointed me and I was more alone. On the one-year anniversary of his leaving, I made a vow that I would never let anyone near my heart again. I wouldn't even let him close.

I thought my tattoo had turned red because my heart was opening.

Now I wonder if it's nothing more than a wound that has yet to heal.

When I can't sleep, I stand at the back door and remember the way things used to be. I think about my family working in the earth and all that the earth gave back to us in return. I look out at the gathering of white doves that were once used to send messages to survivors in the city.

When the doves returned, they came back sightless. They were considered useless after that. But I love the songs they sing. I'm honored that they visit me. When the moon is out and the trees are filled with shining white doves, more beautiful than snow, I walk outside. I climb the tree and sleep among them, listening to the wind.

I wish I could find the answer to my own question. One small bit of truth. I want to know what love is worth. If you can weigh and measure it as my mother once weighed out tomatoes and measured out green beans. I want to know if Diamond is measuring the days since we were last together, or if they mean nothing to him and I alone am counting each hour we're apart.

At night, when I hear my garden growing, I sometimes think I hear something more. I think it's the boy I love, coming back to me. I hear him say my name, even though he was made mute in the fire and I have never heard his voice. In my dreams I hear him say *I'm here with you*. He tells me not to doubt him, or myself, or what we had. But in the mornings, when I wake, I'm alone. The windows of my cottage are covered with vines. I have to pick away the roses one by one.

I have to bleed once more.

There are things in our world that are forever changed, and that is true of me as well. I am still Green, but soon I will turn seventeen, and eighteen is not far off after that. I can't go back to being the girl I once was, any more than the city I loved can rise whole from the ashes. The world is a different, sadder place. The star magnolia trees have blooms again, but the flowers have come back as sharp as glass; they'll prick your fingers if you dare to pick them. The moths that were once white are now black as coal; white moths only exist as a memory. The deer have turned the color of ashes. The doves that were blinded by the flames have fledglings that are sightless from the day they are born, as if their parents' trauma has been bred into their bones.

In town there are rumors that some of us have also been altered in deep, strange ways. The Enchanted — those said to be witches — are those who stood outside for too long while the cinders rained down, or looked at the sun as it gleamed, or drank from the river when it was thick with toxins. People believe in black magic even when there is none. They assume that whatever is different is dangerous — a snake on the road, a toad in the well. They think that my dear neighbor is one of the Enchanted because she lives alone and seeks no one's counsel or love. Aurora and I used to call her a witch and throw apples at her door, but she's just very old, and wiser than most.

There are those who swear that the stones in my neighbor's field can speak and tell the future. They say she is one of the Enchanted, along with a woman who can fly when the moon is full, another who can change her looks the way a chameleon might — beautiful one day, terrifying the next — and yet another who can swim beneath the water, with gills on her neck like a fish.

Of the fifth, they say only that she is a true believer, although in what or in whom, no one seems sure.

There is truth in the notion that we need magic these days.

Certainly we need protection. The people who destroyed the city travel along the river under cover of night, trying to undermine whatever any village may try to repair. We hear explosions while we are asleep in our beds. Our enemies like the way our world is now, without the things they call *the inventions of doom*. On the darkest nights, their soldiers kidnap women who wander off to look for night-flowering quince. They drag away any man who dares to disagree with their way of life, depositing him in a prison from which, it is whispered, no one ever escapes.

These soldiers do not look evil when you come upon them, riding their beautiful black horses.

They have open, handsome faces. They will offer you food, advice, their side of the story. Some of our own people have joined with them, including my schoolmates who had formed the Forgetting Society at a shack in the woods, all of them orphans, all of them lost. My old schoolmates tried to erase their pain with drugs and drink. When they discovered that wasn't possible, despair overcame them. Some ran away or drowned themselves. Some vanished, as my friend Heather had, though I had tried to convince her that even if she was an orphan, she still belonged. A few young people from our village joined the Horde in exchange for a meal, yearning for something to believe in, desperate enough to accept the Horde's philosophy of destruction. They were willing to adhere to one of the Horde's strictest rules.

Should they ever happen upon a book, they were to tear up the pages, soak them with precious kerosene, and let them burn.

In town, our people lock their doors when dusk falls. They board up their windows, blow out the candles. After they say their prayers, they go to sleep with knives beneath their pillows. They never step outside to see the white sliver of the moon in the sky. They haven't noticed that the ash, which obscured the night skies for so long, has drifted away and that we can once again see the stars.

I still work in my garden at night. My mother taught me the best time to harvest is when the moon is in the center of the sky. The best time to plant is when it wanes. I have Onion to protect me. He would bark to alert me if anyone tried to climb the fence that surrounds my garden. The wooden pickets are adorned with glass bottles that sing when the wind blows through. The glass would shatter if anyone dared to sneak in. Not that anyone would. I am far away in the woods. I'm just Green, who can make any garden grow.

Green, who writes stories. Green, who has managed to go on alone.

I've never minded the dark. I can disappear into it, with my green-tattooed skin, my long black hair. I disappear into my stories the very same way. I lose myself inside the ink. I have written about the way the light fell across my mother's face as she told me good-bye, the song my father whistled, the last time Aurora waved to me on that bright morning.

I'm afraid that soon enough there won't be anything more to tell.

There is only one story I want to get to the end of now.

Will he come back to me?

Will I want him if he does?

Today I have my ink and the pen I fashioned from a sharpened hawk feather. I set off with Onion. I have decided to go looking for the Enchanted — if they exist. I want more than just the stories that come to my kitchen, or the ones that follow me down the streets of my town. I want the difficult stories, the ones that aren't easy to believe, the twisted ones, the sorrowful ones, the ones that need telling most of all.

I wear my long green dress for the journey. My feet are bare. I have paper that I specially invented for my neighbor, the one they call a witch. It's made of nettles and shards of rocks. Her paper is heavy. It shimmers like starlight.

Onion runs ahead through the woods. We come upon the three stacks of stones I made to remember and honor my family. A memorial to those I loved and love still. White and silver and black. Moonstones and sunstones and midnight-black stones.

I stop and say what I think is a prayer. I ask for a blessing. I ask to always remember. Then I try to catch up to Onion.

We reach the field of rocks between the woods and my neighbor's house. These are the stones people say can tell a person's future. Although I am no longer caught in the past, the future seems like a ridiculous thing to me. Try to catch it, hold it in your hand. It disappears every time.

I go to knock on my neighbor's door. We have watched over each other in every way we can ever since the city burned down. I deliver food from my garden, and she's brought me closer to understanding the person that I've become. If that's the trick of a witch, then perhaps she is one after all. She was the only person who could help me to see that despite all my loss, I was still myself, still Green at the core.

Are you sure you want to come in? she says, as if there might be something dangerous inside. It's funny, really. I've been here to visit a hundred times. I have spent many Sundays in her parlor. I've washed her windows, brought baskets of yellow and red tomatoes, eaten a birthday cake she baked just for me.

Of course. I laugh. *I want to write down your story.*

Once you write it, you'll know it, she warns me.

I come inside and sit at her table. I write down everything she tells me. How she had been a beautiful young girl whose true love went to war, how she closed down her heart when he never returned. She had watched the world from her window, going no farther than her own stony field. Then one day she woke up and she was old. She had thrown her life away with her mourning. She hadn't known how to go on. She confided that on the burning day, she'd stood unprotected in the firestorm and let the cinders rain down on her. She thought the world was ending and she was ready to have her life be over as well. But it didn't end, and now she can see the future in the rocks in her field. I laugh because I don't believe her.

My neighbor laughs right back. *You think a stone can't save you?*

A year ago, stones had fallen when marauders from the Forgetting Shack tried to take everything in my garden. Someone had come to my rescue, scaring the thieves away. I knew it was my neighbor who had saved me then. But I'd never known why. Now she tells me that she saw herself in me.

She saw past my tattoos to the grief I was trying to cover with ink. She didn't want me to waste my life the way she had wasted so much of hers.

Perhaps she'll help me once more.

I follow her into the field. My sister and I often came here to gather apples. Now there is only brown grass and rocks. After a time, I lean down and pick up a stone. It's green. It seems like mine.

Tell me my future, I say, not thinking she can.

What you are able to dream you are able to grow, she says to me. *If you don't believe in it, it can never happen.*

She tells me to look, insisting my future is within the stone. When I look carefully, I see a leaf inside the rock.

Nothing grows in stone, I say to my neighbor. *It's impossible.*

Just watch, she insists.

We sit there for a long time, until at last the moon rises. Every stone in the field becomes a tree. Every tree is growing taller. I fall asleep because I'm certain I must already be dreaming. But in the morning, when I open my eyes, I'm surrounded by a forest.

In one hand I hold the stone with a leaf inside. In the other there is a leaf with a stone weighing it down.

I take them with me when I go.

Ever since that visit I walk along the river. I think about the way things change, about leaves and stones, about the future. I can't stop myself from wondering about these matters even though I know it's a foolish thing to do. I had taught myself to live in the moment, go day by day, forget about wanting more for myself. But my neighbor had made me wonder what might happen next.

Perhaps that is a kind of witchery, a spell she has cast.

One day as I walk along, I hear something in the distance. I kneel and listen to the earth. Something is brewing. It sounds like a windstorm underground, a change that is to come.

Onion darts off into the woods. I follow, calling. He stops by a cliff of craggy rock. I kneel and listen to the ground again. What I hear now is an echo, like my garden growing, but noisier. It's the sound of machines, something I haven't heard all this past year.

I tie Onion to a tree, tell him to hush, then creep toward the cliff. There is a cave right in front of me. If a bear is inside, so be it. If a monster is there, there's nothing I can do. I'll never know if I don't go to see.

I keep on. It should be dark inside, but it's bright, as if a thousand candles are burning.

There are pieces of metal scattered around: cogs, wheels, nails, wires. Generators and lanterns glow. I realize only one person could have managed all this. I have entered the workshop of the Finder. I feel awed that someone has gathered together so much of our past. His back is to me as he works, but when he hears me he turns, an arrow in a bow aimed at my heart.

Despite the threat, I laugh when I see him. He's only a boy. Thirteen at most. He looks familiar. He's probably someone who was several grades behind me in school. A boy to whom I never paid much attention. Someone my sister might have known.

No one is allowed here, he tells me.

For someone so young, he's very sure of himself. The king of the junkyard, of all that was lost.

I recognize him then. He'd been a nervous boy, a prize student, too shy to speak in front of anyone. His sister had done all his talking for him, as mine had once done for me.

His sister was Heather Jones. The girl I'd tried and failed to save.

I know you, I say. *You're Troy Jones.*

He still has the arrow pointed at me. But he seems hesitant once I call him by name. Still, a boy playing with a dangerous toy can be dangerous himself.

I knew your sister, I say. *Heather was my friend.*

Now that he realizes who I am, he puts down the bow. *I've heard about you. You're the one who writes stories. I made something for you. I thought you might come by someday. You look for stories the way I look for machine parts.*

He's rebuilt a typewriter for me. It's made of mismatched pieces, with clackety old keys and leather straps I can use to carry it like a backpack. It is the best gift anyone has ever given me.

Why would you do this? I want to know.

There's something I can't find, Troy Jones admits. *Something I need from you.*

Impossible. I've heard you can find anything.

He shakes his head sadly. *I can't find Heather.*

He had only one sister, as had I. He's an orphan now, too.

I sit him down and tell him his sister has disappeared. When I'd gone to look for her, all that had remained were a few scraps of a blue dress near a fire pit. I'd given her the dress; it had belonged to my mother and it had been beautiful. I tell Troy that Heather is gone and there is no sense in searching for her.

Troy insists I'm wrong. He has a camera, the only one in our village. He found packets of film that raise images as if by magic. He has taken some snapshots he wants me to see. They're grainy and dark but I manage to make out the images. There is my friend Heather — just a fleeting glimpse, but Heather all the same. She is caught in the stoptime of the camera as one of the Horde lifts her onto his black horse. The dress Heather wears is a ragged blue. It's the dress my mother had worn to dances when the world was different. Now, like a miracle, it appears once more.

I ran after them, but I couldn't catch up, Troy tells me. *People say one of the Enchanted can tell you how to find your heart's desire. I know you've set out to collect their stories. All I want is to know where my sister is now. I want you to collect that for me.*

I've heard the same idle gossip. One of the Enchanted is said to see the future, one can see disaster, one can see true love, one can save you, one was a believer. People guess which among them could grant you your heart's desire. It has become a game children chant when they jump rope.

Stone, Sky, Rose, River, Earth.
Let me know just what I'm worth.
Tell me where my true love can be found.
In the sky, the flowers, the river, or deep in the ground.

I've tried every other way to find Heather. Troy's voice is insistent. *Now I need you.*

Why me? I want to know.

Because the Enchanted will talk to you. They'll tell you their stories.

I thought that what you lost you could never get back. I thought I knew the end of most stories. But I was wrong.

I spy a magnifying glass on the worktable. I grab it, then take a closer look at the photograph. My hands are shaking. The half of my tattooed heart feels the way it had when the first needle went in. Like ice. Like heat. As though it had begun beating.

I thought I recognized the denim jacket worn by one of the Horde riders.

Now, upon a closer look, I do.

It's the person whose story I want most of all, the boy who appeared in my garden, the one who'd gone in search of his family, only to disappear.

Diamond.

The boy I loved.

I don't turn on the lantern that night. I sit alone in my house, in the darkness, my sister's dog beneath the table. I can hear crickets in the garden. I hear moths at the windowpanes. Troy Jones asked for my help because he believes I can hear what no one else can. A cry in the distance. A heart that beats when all else is still. He is convinced that people will tell me their stories, and in those stories we'll find what we're looking for. Lies, after all, can be unearthed in many places. But the truth is much harder to decipher, on this we agree.

There's only one way to know if he's right.

I must find out for myself.

Sky

Witch

This is what I learned

What you see, you can understand.

Someone once told me this, but I laughed out loud.

I said I had seen smoke and ashes and death and I didn't understand any of it. I had seen love as well, and that had turned out to be the biggest mystery of all.

But I had looked at the outside of things, not at the true, ever-changing heart. Look at a cloud and see how it becomes a swan, a rose, a lantern, a lion. That is the only way to understand that all clouds change.

Not a single one can ever stay the same.

That doesn't mean it's not still a cloud.

The Enchanted never allow themselves to be known. They don't wish to be made into goddesses or demons. They are merely women who have suffered. They want to be left alone. They know what happens to witches in this world. Every little girl does.

Because they won't reveal themselves or deny their existence, people tell lies. But a lie is not a story, it's simply a lie. Lies become bigger, and fatter, and meaner every time they're told. They eat air and inflate with each piece of gossip. They feel real, but when you touch them, they pop like a bubble. There's nothing inside.

People have begun to say that the Enchanted steal children and keep them in cages. They cast spells in which dogs become men and men become dogs. They turn women into birds, fish, stones, thorns, hedges, monsters.

The townspeople whisper that the witch who can fly sleeps in a nest; she lays eggs and has feathers and talons. They say she knows things a flesh-and-blood woman has no business knowing. She knows your thoughts, your deepest despair, your brightest hope. She can call you by your given name even though she's never seen you before. If you aren't careful, she gets inside your mind. She understands you better than you understand yourself, seeing through to your truest self, whether you like it or not.

Hers is the first story I want to hear.

I start down the road with Onion and a basket of food, the typewriter strapped to my back. The packet of paper I made is stored in a mesh bag I use for drying herbs and sometimes for carrying Onion when he grows tired. I walk for miles under a cloudless sky. I like the feel of the road under my feet, I like the fresh air, but I don't like my own fears. What if the whispers are true? What if the last thing a witch wants is to tell her own story?

Clouds begin to appear in the east as if to echo my cloudy thoughts. They form a tower, a heart, a ring, a bird without wings.

Diamond left me to find his mother and his people. But what if his people are our enemies? What if I hadn't seen him for who he really was? What if our love is something I'd only imagined, yearned for, invented out of air?

My journey takes a day and a night. At last, I see the high tower where the Sky Witch lives. It was once a fire tower. A fire marshal watched over our valley from this vantage point, on the lookout for the signs of smoke. But there is no longer a fire brigade. All our firemen went to the city on the day of the disaster, and they never returned. They crossed the bridge in a desperate attempt to save whoever might be left, but the flames leapt higher and the bridge collapsed behind them.

These men can't be replaced. Not ever.

Now if something is set on fire, our people simply stand and watch it burn.

I pop Onion into the mesh bag, then begin up the rickety ladder. I climb higher and higher, past the tops of the trees, right through a cloud. It's so high I don't dare to look down. I'm breathless, afraid I might fall. But I keep on. I'm at the point where going forward is easier than going back.

I don't stop until I see her. Of course she knew I was coming. She probably knew before I did. She has set out a bowl of water for Onion and a pot of tea made of berries and herbs for me. The tea is blue, hot and salty, like tears. The first sip is so bitter I nearly choke.

You'll get used to the taste, she tells me. And true enough, I do.

The woman who lives in the tower, the one

people swear has feathers and claws, was once the mother of six children. Now she is all alone in a nest made of twigs on the highest platform of the fire tower. The air here is cold and thin and clear. The wind makes you shiver, the sun makes you burn.

The woman in the tower has hair that is knotted with blue feathers; her dress is woven from the down of blue jays. When she sings, the air fills with birds of every variety. Orioles, mockingbirds, nightingales, kestrels — varieties I haven't seen since the city burned down. There are hummingbirds, herons, snowy owls, even parakeets and canaries that have escaped from their cages.

I spy a hawk, one I saved after the fire. He's perched on the roof of the tower — a guard keeping watch over our valley. I had cared for his burns with my mother's lotions and salves. I nursed him back to health and watched him fly away when he was healed.

He looks beautiful here, so high above the world, so at home in the sky.

I'm so happy to see him.

When I tell the woman who lives in the tower I've come to write down her story, she doesn't seem surprised. She doesn't shout or insist I leave as I feared she might. Troy Jones was right. She wants to tell me her story. She actually seems impatient, as if she has been waiting to reveal it for a long time. She speaks so quickly it's not easy to keep up with her. It's like trying to type the wind. She has cried so many tears over the past year that the leaves on the trees beneath the tower have all turned blue. It looks as if there is only sky below us, so vast and endless we can never get back to the ground.

I feel dizzy, but I keep writing. I am still Green, the one who will listen to your story. Green, the searcher. Green, looking for my heart's desire.

The woman in the tower hasn't spoken much since the disaster. At first her words sound like birdsongs, but after a while I understand. She had been asleep with her children when the accident happened, all of them safe and napping in their beds, nestled in a house on the hill. Her husband had been one of the firemen who raced across the bridge before it fell. His name was Jack Bird. Her husband's name sounds like a song in her mouth. She cannot measure his courage.

But can you measure someone's love? I want to know.

You think you can measure love?

She's kind not to laugh at me. I must seem a fool, a girl named Green who doesn't yet understand the world.

No scale would be strong enough, she tells me. *It would break to pieces under the weight.*

On that terrible day, the firestorm ripped through her house in a blinding light. When she opened her eyes, she was alone. Her children had been turned into piles of ash. Her house was destroyed, but she stayed, unprotected from the fallout, the rain, the torrents of leaves, the moths and bats. She slept under a sky that was black at noon. She couldn't leave her children even though people insisted they were no longer there. A group of kindhearted women from town came to comfort her, but she wouldn't even look at them, let alone allow herself to be brought into the village.

Then one day the wind rose up, and the piles of ash that had been her children rose up as well, into the sky, higher and higher. She ran after them, desperate, trying her best to catch up. She went through the woods, past the river, along the road, until she came to this place. She has been here ever since, watching out over the country-side, exactly as her husband, Jack Bird, had done when he was the fire marshal, before he raced into the city on that burning day.

All her life she had been happy but foolish, she tells me. She had been too busy with the small details of her own life to appreciate what she had. She couldn't even remember if she'd kissed her husband good-bye on that last day, or if she had sung her children to sleep before she tucked them in for their naps.

Now she keeps watch over our valley with the help of the hawk. Lately, her eyes have been watering. There has been smoke. The Horde is going from town to town with their torches. They're coming closer to our village.

From up here I see everything, the woman in the tower tells me.

She is nothing like the gossips suggested, not a birdwoman with talons and a beak, squawking and wheeling across the sky. Just the mother of lost children with feathers in her hair.

What you see, you can understand, she says.

I don't believe that, I tell her. I still can't make sense of anything I've seen.

Look at it from the inside, she tells me.

On that terrible day, she had gazed up into the sky for too long, staring straight into the burning black sun. She had lost her children and her brave husband. It seemed she had nothing more to lose, but she had.

Only then do I realize that her eyes are milky. She has lost her sight. She's a blind woman keeping watch over our village, our valley, our lives. Still, her lack of vision doesn't keep her from knowing what our future might bring.

I can tell they're coming closer because of the birds, she tells me.

She hands me a single blue feather, which I slip into my pocket alongside the stone that contains a leaf.

Every day more flocks of birds come to our valley, she says.

They're being chased out of the woods by the fires soldiers from the Horde are setting in villages along the river. Each time the attackers ride in on their black horses, more people are captured and brought to their prison.

Can you grant a heart's desire? I ask. I'm asking as

much for myself as I am for Troy Jones. *Can you find someone who's been lost?*

Someone may be able to, but it's not me, she says sadly. *I can only tell you about what I lost. I can only tell you my story.*

When I write her story, I record the names of all her children and everything they had loved. Jonah had loved apples and William had loved trucks. Sarah had loved books and Melinda had loved hopping about in the rain and Loren had loved rolling in the grass. The littlest of all, the baby named Sam, had loved waking up in the morning and seeing the color of the sky. The paper I use for her has feathers mixed in. The color is a pure pale blue. It looks like spirit paper, cloudy, sky-tinged, as though it's been saturated with tears.

By the time the story is told, it's late and I've grown tired. The woman in the sky lets me stay overnight in the tower. I'm not bothered by the height anymore. All night the wind blows and the woman who lost her children keeps watch. She never sleeps. She is beyond sleep, she confides, day and night are one and the same. But I sleep deeply for the first time in a very long time. I don't worry that my garden may be growing over the windows and doors. That night I dream of six stars in the sky and six birds in a nest. I dream about a baby who loved gardens and green living things.

When I wake just before dawn, I'm alone, the dog sleeping at my feet, the clouds all around me. The woman with no children is gone. I notice there is blue fabric woven into the nest.

I think of Heather Jones.

I think of Diamond.

I try to see with my heart and not only with my eyes. I gaze out and try to look beyond what's right in front of me.

There are flocks of birds in the distance. The blind doves that often nest in my garden are reeling through the air. Among them is one blue-bird flying straight into the wind, higher than all the rest. Her shape is the form of a woman. She perches on the roofs of houses in our village to sing children to sleep with lullabies. She keeps watch all night long, making certain no one's house burns down in the dark and no one else's children are lost.

When the morning breaks open into bands of clear light, I can see farther than I ever have before, all the way along the river. This tower is the highest point for miles around, and the landscape is like a quilt stretched out before me. Villages and fields and woods are a hodgepodge of yellow and green. I see windmills and roads and roses and houses. In the distance, on the other side of the river, lies the city. From here it still looks beautiful, as it did when it was made out of silver and gold.

Then I notice something I've never seen before. In the center of the river there is an island where an old prison once stood. The prison is well hidden by shrubs and vines. You can't see it from our village, only from up here in the sky. This is where the Horde takes men who won't give up the future, and women who refuse to step back into a time when they had no words and no rights.

From this distance the prison looks like a castle. Smoke spirals from the watchtowers. Skulls are nailed to the cornice stones. I spy a flag of ragged blue fabric waving in one window. To me it looks like a flag made of tears.

The flag disappears after only a moment, but I have seen it. A sign from Heather Jones. I'm sure of it. But where is the person I had loved, the boy who gave me my heart, then broke it in two?

Where is Diamond?

I walk home thinking about things I thought I was done with. Love, loyalty, lies. It rains and the rain is green. When I reach my gate, I see that my garden has grown even taller. I cut a path through the twisted wisteria, the blood red roses, the beans on vines that reach all the way to the chimney top.

After I feed Onion, I work on the books I've written, sewing the pages together. I use vines as my thread, thorns as my needles. I have a bookcase full of stories now. The baker's story smells like cinnamon. The scientist's story has the scent of grass. My teacher's tale of the books she loved has stray words that fall out when I turn the pages. *Heath* and *desire* and *moors.* My neighbor with the field of stones has a book so heavy it nearly breaks the shelf in two.

When the book for the woman who lost her children is done, it's so light I have to tie it to the floor to stop it from rising up to the ceiling.

That week when I trek into town with my wheelbarrow of vegetables, Onion follows along, barking at everyone we pass. I notice that the children in the village are singing the lullaby, the one they'd heard in their dreams. I think about the Enchanted. I wonder why it is that those who are the most wounded can often see what others cannot.

More than ever I want their stories on my bookcase.

I want them to last.

The Finder soon comes to see me. I'm easy to locate. You don't need much talent to find me. I'm planting red snap peas in my garden on a dark night. Because I'm still thinking about Diamond, the beans are all turning red. When people in the village eat them, they'll dream of kisses. They'll want to go out looking for love.

The moon is hidden behind clouds, but the weather is warm. It's late spring. Soon enough I'll be turning seventeen. Somehow that seems old to me. So much has happened. So much is gone. I'm lonely in a way I don't understand. I feel like one of the black moths flitting around a lantern, looking for the moon and finding only a false light, burning its wings in the process.

When the Finder appears, Onion doesn't growl. Troy Jones wants to know if I found the witch who can grant a heart's desire. I shake my head.

I tell him what I saw from the tower, the island prison in the center of the river. The skulls and the smoke and the blue flag.

I had believed that Heather had fallen asleep near the fire. I thought she'd been burned to ashes. I presumed I knew her story, but I'd been wrong. Now I wonder if perhaps you can't know the end of something until you get there.

We go inside and have a meal of tomato soup and nettle bread. I serve Troy a slice of cake made from pumpkin seeds and chestnut flour. It's my mother's recipe, so of course it's delicious. He wolfs down the cake, then politely asks for more. I know he's thinking about everything I've told him, and thinking makes him hungry. He's only a boy, after all, still growing. In time he will be tall — six feet tall, maybe more.

As he eats the pumpkin cake, Troy tells me he became the Finder by accident. When he began to search for his sister, he discovered so many other things our village needed. He reminds me that his father had been a carpenter. Troy himself was always a tinkerer by nature. He's good at puzzles and can easily put most contraptions together. He tells me this is why he has decided to go to the prison. If his sister is there, he's certain he can help her escape.

I'm not so certain. Surely, he will be seen as a threat. If he goes to the prison in search of Heather, he will most likely be caught and arrested, perhaps locked up for years. But a girl who is a mere weed can slip in and out of the dark. That's what's needed. Someone no one will notice. Someone who can find Heather.

Someone like me.

I convince Troy, and yet I still have doubts. I spied the blue flag in the prison window, but I don't have faith in my own vision. Perhaps it was only a shadow, a cloud, a blue jay in the far distance. Who am I to leave my garden and go in search of anything? For that you need a believer, and that isn't me. You need someone who is certain the future is a possibility, who is convinced that lost things can be found.

I wish my mother, who always offered such good advice, was here to tell me what to do. I wish my father, who was always so strong, could go and kick down the prison gates. I wish my sister, with her open nature, could remind me to follow my own heart, a heart I'm not even sure I have anymore.

Troy insists he can convince me there is something for me to find. *All you need do is open your eyes and look*, he tells me. He brings a small wooden box out of his pocket, the kind that is often tied to the leg of a dove to send messages into the city.

It must have fallen off one of the doves nesting in your

tree. It was right in your garden but you didn't see it, Troy tells me.

I probably walked past it scores of times. But I never once spied it there in the grass.

I slide open the cover of the little wooden message box. Inside there is a tiny painting. I feel a tightness in my chest. Diamond had been a painter. Even when he couldn't speak, he could show me how he felt through his paintings.

When I unroll the scrap of canvas, I see my own face. But the face is beautiful. I know I don't look like that. Except, perhaps, in the eyes of someone who loves me.

On the back of the painting, half a heart has been painted in red.

The half he took with him when he left.

Look at the mark on the box, Troy tells me.

It's a prison stamp. A small black skull, like the ones nailed to the tower, the ones I'd seen from my perch in the sky.

Is Diamond a prisoner or a guard? Is he my worst enemy or still my beloved? Can I find anything, or simply lose more?

I must have spoken aloud. I must need an answer. The Finder is happy to oblige.

That's for you to find out, Troy Jones says.

We leave the next morning.

Rose
Witch

This is what I hoped

What you look for, you may find.

Someone promised me this, but I shook my head.

I insisted that what was lost was gone forever.
I believed that *searcher* was simply another name
for *fool*.

I had made a life for myself in the village. I
had gone on despite my sorrow, difficult as that
was. It should have been enough to wake up every
day, to see the roses in my garden, to know I was

alive. Surely, wanting more would only bring more despair.

But desire can drive you for miles. It can lead you in ways you never would have imagined. A map can be written in ashes, earth, water, air. Take a step and keep walking. Don't be afraid to look back.

In the end, every path you choose takes you closer to what you've been searching for all along.

Troy and I set off together. I tell him that I've heard that the Rose Witch likes gifts. People say she's vain and silly, a greedy, foolish woman. But no one can agree on a description. How she looks seems to depend on the viewer. The grocery owner's wife, who had once delivered food to her cottage, told me that the woman who lived there was so ugly she had run away without being paid, something I had difficulty believing.

On the other hand, Uncle Tim vows she is the most beautiful woman he's ever seen. He was wandering through a meadow with his dogs when he spied her. He swore her long hair was the color of roses. But of course he had been far away, and the witch disappeared when she noticed him, her own dog at her heels.

The children who play in the town square say that whenever they leave flowers beside her road, she repays them by setting out little cakes that taste like pistachio or almond. If you bring her roses, she gives out special chocolates, the kind we never see anymore, with cherry-red centers.

The children don't believe she is a witch at all.

The toll-taker at the bridge stopped by one day just to give me his opinion. He was shy, and I waited for him to tell me what he thought. He saw the witch in his own way. The Rose Witch could be a hundred different women with a hundred different faces, if what everyone says is true.

The toll-taker told me the Rose Witch was so lovely that she would entrance men on their way to the bridge. He swore he'd seen it time and again — but of course from a distance, like all the rest. Men would give up everything for her and follow her home. Only then did she reveal herself to be a monster. I noticed the toll-taker's glasses were broken. He had to squint when he looked across the table to see my face. I wondered if he saw monsters where there were none. If everyone's inner vision decided who the Rose Witch was.

As for me, I believe that even a monster has a story to tell, so I bring along extra paper. I've used rose water so that the pages are tinged with flecks of crimson. I added a handful of red petals. For some reason this paper made me cry when I cut it into sheets. It was as though I had mixed up true love without even trying. Bees hovered over the kettle, as if there was honey inside. There hadn't been bees in our part of the world for a long time. I took their return as a sign of good luck.

On our journey I carry my typewriter on my back. I am bringing an armful of my most beautiful roses, some of them as big as cabbages. They are the best things I have to offer. Onion follows and Troy Jones leads the way.

We stop to pay our respects at the stone monuments I built for my family. We stand quietly in the middle of the woods and bow our heads. I wonder if you ever miss people any less. I would trade anything to have one word from my mother, one hug from my father, one day to run through the fields with my sister.

Onion is well behaved for once, but as soon as we leave the stacks of stones and head for the road, he races out in front, flushing rabbits from their hiding places, although he's never quick enough to catch one.

The bees follow along, drawn by the huge red roses I'm holding. In no time there is a stream of bees humming like mad. When we can see the bridge, I feel a lump in my throat. I still don't think I will ever walk across it. I look at it, spanning the river, and all I can remember is that day. I remember I was the selfish girl who stayed home. I still wake up every morning though the others are gone. I still bleed. I breathe. I alone have gone on.

There is still very little traffic in and out of the city, perhaps one traveler a day. When the toll-taker spies us, he waves from his booth. We are too far away for him to see clearly, and I don't think he recognizes us. From this distance, how can he tell who is a monster and who is beautiful?

I stick out my tongue to test him, but the toll-taker just keeps waving, friendly as ever. Troy and I laugh. Clearly, that man can't see a thing.

There is the road off to the side, one you might walk right by if you weren't searching for something. We stop laughing. The witch's road is lined with dead things. Brambles. Black trees. Stalks of belladonna and hazel and thorn apple. Skeletons of mice and raccoons and rabbits that were burned alive. These fields suffered from some of the worst of the fires. After all this time, the soil is still hot. I am grateful I decided to wear my boots. I put Onion into the mesh bag and carry him so he won't burn his paws.

I thought the bees would flee, but they follow along. Troy Jones has brought a sword. Just in case. But instead of enemies we have found brambles. Troy looks like a boy playing at war. If our world hadn't been changed, that's what he might be. But now he is the Finder. He puts the sword to good use. He cuts down all the dead growth. When he's done, I lean down and put my hands into the earth. I can feel the beginning of something. As we walk on, the vines unfold behind us. The witch hazel blooms with yellow flowers. Meadowlarks crisscross the sky. We can barely hear each other over the thrumming of the bees. I can't make out what Troy says to me. He looks worried. He points to the house at the end of the path.

There is a woman waiting for us in her doorway.

Maybe we should go back, Troy Jones says now.

All this talk of witches has made him nervous. He's a thirteen-year-old boy who'd been on his own since the day of the fire. Of course he's mistrustful. Anyone would be. But I'm not about to turn away now. I have spied a dog on the porch, a big white greyhound, one I had rescued after the fire. I'd helped to heal her burned paws, then set her free to find her home. I'd called her Ghost because she had appeared in the woods one day, so quiet she was like mist drifting between the trees. Now she runs to us, then leaps to greet me.

I'm so happy to see her.

Come on, then, the woman in the doorway calls when she sees that her dog welcomes us. *Unless you're afraid.*

From this distance she might be beautiful or she might be a monster. I understand all the confusion now. Truly, it's impossible to tell. You have to look from the inside out.

We're here to see you. Whoever you turn out to be, I call back.

This must be the right thing to say, because she waves us on.

As we approach we see that she's just a woman with red hair who had been burned in the fire. Sparks had fallen on her face and left their mark. I present the roses, which she arranges in a vase. She has beautiful hands and a sweet speaking voice.

I explain that we are searching for Troy's sister.

Is there anything else you're searching for? the red-haired woman asks me.

There's something about her that makes me think of true love. The truth slips out before I can stop myself.

There's someone named Diamond, I admit.

She takes us through her back door. A single white rosebush grows there, surrounded by a field of black ashes.

The woman stops me. She puts one hand on my arm.

Before you go any farther you should know one thing: What you look for, you may find.

I had thought there wasn't anything to find behind her house other than a ruined field where nothing could grow. I thought true love was something I had only imagined.

But when I look past the roses I see the island where the prisoners are kept. There are the turrets, there are the skulls. A blue flag hangs in a window, wound through the metal bars. A dozen white doves circle the tower, the same ones that nested in my garden. A trail of white rose trees frames a path that will take us to the riverbank.

It's growing dark. We ask if we can spend the night before we set out on the path of ashes. We still have a long way to go. While Troy sleeps on the couch in the parlor, I set up my typewriter. When I take out the paper I made, I realize it has changed. The rose petals I added have turned from red to white. The paper has become smooth as silk. It smells of rose water and sulfur, a combination that could make anyone cry.

The red-haired woman is ready to tell me her story. The accident happened on her wedding day. She had wanted everything to be perfect, so she told her guests to go ahead into the city. All her family, her friends, the groom.

Don't take too long, her beloved had said.

But she did. She took her time. She wanted the day to last forever. She wanted everything to be just right. She washed her hair with perfumed soap and made her own bouquet with two dozen white roses plucked from the hedge outside her door. Her dress was made of silk — she'd sewn it herself, adding the beads and pearls. She took an iron and lovingly pressed out each wrinkle.

By the time she was ready, she was extremely late. She had to run, her dog at her side. She saw her groom on the bridge, signaling for her to hurry. There was a crowd and she couldn't get through. All of a sudden the bridge wasn't there anymore. There was nothing but fire. Her dress turned red. Her hair turned red. The roses in her hands turned reddest of all, consumed by the flame. Her dog ran off and barked for her to follow. But she wouldn't leave. She wouldn't turn away. She watched the bridge sink into the water. The tears she cried burned themselves into her face, leaving their marks in her skin.

By the time she turned away, everything was gone.

A single petal from the roses I've brought her falls onto the table. It's turned a pure white. I think of my garden in winter. I think of Diamond.

You wanted to know how heavy love is? she says. *So light you can carry it your whole life long.*

Can you grant a heart's desire? I ask her then.

Oh, she says. She seems surprised. She looks at me carefully. *Aren't you Green?*

I nod. That's me. Green, who writes down stories, who still doesn't know the truth about love. Green, who pricks her fingers on roses yet never cries. Green, who is still searching for things she doesn't believe she can ever find.

The woman who had almost been a bride is sadder than ever.

I had hoped you would do that for me, she sighs.

That night I can't sleep. I take Ghost and Onion for a walk. The bees are still in the meadow, still rumbling. Everywhere Troy cut down the brambles, everywhere I'd put my hands into the earth, the plants are growing so fast I can see leaves unfolding in the dark. There are apple trees and stalks of new grass.

I am still Green, who has a talent in the garden. Green, who can make nearly anything bloom. But that doesn't mean I can grant a heart's desire. For me, half a heart is painful enough.

The dogs have run off into the darkness and now I have to search for them. I whistle, but they don't come running back. At last I find them in the campground where Uncle Tim keeps the town's abandoned dogs. There are dozens of them, but I spot Ghost and Onion right away.

Uncle Tim is so lonely that he's grateful for the opportunity to walk me back to the road, his band of strays charging ahead. He tells me stories about his life in the city. He'd been a gardener. He'd found great pleasure in bringing green things to life on city streets, where there would have been only cobblestones and bricks had it not been for him.

When we turn onto the witch's road, Uncle Tim grins. He notices the humming in the fields. He says bees always mean a garden is beginning.

That is a fact, he says. *Gardens are stronger than buildings. They bloom when everything else is gone.*

The red-haired woman is waiting for us. From this distance she looks like a dream. She looks like a photograph taken in the past, trapped behind the meshing of her screen door. She seems uncertain about stepping out. I understand only too well. When you are the sole survivor of anything, do you have the right to be alive? Is the future a betrayal of everyone you ever loved and lost, or is it a way to praise them?

The greyhound and Onion run to the red-haired woman. Uncle Tim's dogs race to her as well, even though several of them are usually standoffish.

That's the beautiful woman I told you about, Tim whispers.

We walk up to the house together and I introduce them. Uncle Tim bows.

At last, he says to the woman inside, delighted to have found her.

I catch the scent of sulfur and burning sugar in the air. I think about the red snap peas I planted in my garden that will taste like kisses.

The red-haired woman opens her door, but she hesitates.

Are you sure you want to come inside? she asks Tim. *Some people say there's a monster in my house.*

He gazes inside. There are the roses in a vase on the table. The Finder is curled up on the couch. Asleep, he seems even younger than his age. A boy who in another world might have been a student, played at war, had a family to watch over him.

Tim laughs. *That's only Troy Jones*, he jokes. *I know him. He's a good boy, not a monster.*

Look at me, the red-haired woman demands. Her voice sounds like heartbreak. *Look carefully.*

With pleasure, Uncle Tim replies. He is younger than I'd first thought. He's so kindhearted no dog has ever barked at him. No child has ever cried in front of him. No bee has ever tried to sting him.

I sit on the floor with the dogs while Tim and the red-haired woman have tea. It's a mixture of rose hips, rose petals, and rose leaves. It must be delicious because they share cup after cup. I don't think they remember that I'm there.

I realize I'm watching the way love begins.

Would you like me to tell your future? the red-haired woman asks Tim.

She sounds uneasy. Perhaps it's a trick question, a way to find out if Uncle Tim thinks the future is a far-off, unreachable country. One in which she doesn't belong.

Why don't you tell me tomorrow when you come to visit me? Tim says before he sets out for home with his dogs. *Come early, so our future together can begin.*

After he leaves, the red-haired woman and I sit out on the porch. We can hear Uncle Tim whistling. We're both thinking about love but we don't discuss it. We just want to think about it in the darkness of the night. Even when we can't hear Tim whistling anymore, we can still hear the bees in the field.

I never thought a map could be made out of roses. I never thought the sound of bees could be so beautiful. In the dark, the marks on the red-haired woman's face look more like white stars than like teardrops or burns.

In the morning when I wake, she's already

gone. She's taken her dog with her, the big white greyhound I'd once set free to find a true home. But she's left an envelope for me on the table.

Inside is a single rose petal.

It's the only map I need.

River
Witch

This is who I searched for

Someone once told me that love is an act of will.

I was certain I'd heard wrong.

    I thought that love was a river, endless and deep. I thought it merely happened, washing over you like water. It was nothing to search for, nothing to force. I didn't understand that even when we can't control our fate, we alone have the last say in matters of the heart. We can give it freely, even in the worst of times, even when it isn't returned.

The frightened walk away when love is difficult. I know that now. You have to be willing to give everything away. You have to be willing to end up with nothing.

Only then will your heart be whole.

The Finder and I go down to the muddy banks of the river, trekking through the marshes. We pass by toads, snakes, and a strange breed of walking fish that had been forever changed on the day of the accident. But the river is much clearer now. Minnows dart through the shallows. Water lilies appear in our wake, pale green pads with trailing vines and moon-colored flowers. They make me think of my sister, Aurora. I can't help but wonder if it might be true that for every step you take, everyone you've ever loved walks with you.

Two sparrows fly above us. They don't seem the least bit afraid of us. I believe they might be fledglings I rescued after the fire. Sure enough, when I hold out my arm, they light in the palm of my hand. They are so full of life I can feel their hearts beating. Even after they dart off, they circle back to make sure we're still following. They skirt the brambles artfully, utterly comfortable in the air.

I'm so happy to see them.

The sparrows lead us to the edge of the river where there is a cottage made out of an old boat. Troy Jones loves old broken things. He announces that he thinks it's the most beautiful house in the world. Maybe he's right. It certainly is one of a kind. Instead of windows, there are portholes. Instead of a roof, there's a white sail. Every time the wind rises, the house pulls toward the river, as if it yearns to be sailing, as if a house could have its own heart's desire.

A dock trails out into the water. An old woman is there, a lantern beside her. She looks at least a hundred years old. She is the River Witch. Once she had been a fisherman's wife. Now she wears a black shawl.

If she has gills like a fish, the way people

whisper she does, we can't see them. If her skin is made of scales, as the fearful insist, we can't tell. To us she merely looks like a fisherman's wife who has become a widow.

When I ask the River Witch if I can write down her story, she nods. I have added blue fish scales and water lilies to her paper. It shimmers like water, iridescent in the sunlight. But the back of the paper is brown and murky, like the river when it is flooding, when no one can control the way it flows.

Once, the fisherman's wife had only been aware of all she did not have — she wanted a big house, a child, a life in which her husband did not leave her alone for weeks while he sailed down the river to the sea. When the fisherman made his boat into a house so she could travel with him, she had been disappointed. When he brought her bracelets and rings from far-off lands, she never satisfied. The fisherman was so kindly he could not pass by someone's despair without trying to lend a hand. The fisherman's wife told him that he did too little for her and too much for others. He was always the first to help a stranger, rescue a drowning man, and that is what he did on the day the city burned down. He went out in a rowboat time after time, fishing out those who were swimming away from the fires to save their lives. The last time he went out, he didn't return.

I didn't know his worth, the old woman tells me. *Until it was too late.*

He washed up onshore ten days later, and ever since that time she has not moved from her place on the dock. She has been waiting for a reason to move. She will not leave this place until she can find a way to help others, as her husband once did.

The fisherman's wife invites us to sit beside her. I wonder how she's managed to survive. Why hasn't she starved? She tells me the sparrows bring her bits of fruit and seeds. That is enough to sustain her.

But why do this? I ask.

The fisherman's wife whispers. What she recounts is for my ears alone.

Because love is an act of will. You think it will just happen, but you have to make it so. Even when it's gone wrong. Wait and see. If love doesn't come to you, you have to go find it.

From the dock we can see the prison. There is the blue flag. There are the skulls. So close by, but because of the river between us, so far away. The soldiers of the Horde leave their horses in a pasture on our side of the river and use an old barge to go back and forth to the island.

I recall the photograph of Diamond riding one of those black horses. I feel angry and hurt, then I think of what the fisherman's wife has told me. I will myself to wait, just as the fisherman's wife sits on the dock, waiting.

I will not run away before I know the end of the story.

Since she has been sitting in the same place for so long, the fisherman's wife knows more about the Horde than anyone. She's been watching patiently the way a fisherman patiently waits for the biggest fish.

The news she has is grim.

The Horde, she says, *gathers much the way they gathered before burning down the city.*

This time, however, their eyes are on us. The villagers.

Not again, I think. *Not us.*

I ask how she can be sure. She says she's seen them stockpiling barrels of gunpowder. She's overheard soldiers discussing their battle plans.

It makes sense that they would come after us. We have the Finder. We have generators and windmills. The future is ahead of us. We have been starting over.

We have to go back and warn people that the Horde is on the way, Troy says.

No, I say. I feel certain of what we must do next. *We have to stop them.*

The old woman of the river agrees. *While they are gathering for the attack, they have left their prisoners nearly unguarded. You must empty their prison and bring them defeat.*

They are holding at least a hundred prisoners. How can we bring them back to shore? How can we rescue them?

The fisherman's wife surprises us by rising from her place on the dock.

I finally have a reason to move, she tells us. *I'll help you in every way I can.*

She walks slowly along the dock, then up a path made of fish bones. She has been in one place for so long she has to relearn how to walk. We try to help her, but she tells us that some things must be shared and some must be done alone.

When we reach the end of the fish-bone path, she shows us two large wooden levers on the porch of her house. Her husband had been a tinkerer, like Troy. He liked puzzles as much as he liked boats. If the levers are pulled, the house can be pushed into the river. It will be again what it had been before it was their house: a huge sailing ship.

Troy finds the planking the fisherman had once used to slip the boat into the water.

Now I know it was our dreamhouse, the fisherman's wife says. *When we slept together in bed, we dreamed of oceans, starfish, lagoons.*

She takes a fishhook from her pocket. It's small. It looks light, but when she places it in my hand, it is surprisingly heavy.

This is how much love weighs, she tells me. *Nothing if you don't take it when it's offered. Everything if you accept what's given to you.*

We get on board and wait for the tide to rise. The world seems quiet, yet anything seems possible. The fisherman's wife knows how to work the rigging. At last she has a reason to leave her dock, because we need her help. She has a reason to live again.

In the dark we edge toward the island. As we draw close we hear frogs, night birds, waves against the shore. We hear the Horde speaking in a language we don't understand, just as we never understood how they could be so certain that heaven is on their side, that they alone have the right to chart what is a sin. For them, the past is the only marker. The future is nothing but dangerous territory. The death of innocent people is a price they're willing to pay in order to build their vision of heaven on earth.

There is no language that can give a reasonable voice to that.

When I consider the Horde and the prison before us, I'm frightened. Then I think about my sister in the green market in the city just before the fire began, unaware that it was her last day on earth. There were blue skies, sunlight, crowds of people buying lettuce and peas. It should have been just another day, but it wasn't. It should have been me, if I'd gone instead.

I am thinking about Aurora so deeply I can feel her beside me. I'm not as alone as I'd feared. A year has passed, and although I'm different, she is still the same. She will always be my little sister. I close my eyes and will myself to remember. The apples we picked, the songs we sang, the color of her hair, the way she would sleep on the floor with her little dog. I remember it all. If she were with me, my wild, fearless sister would say I have nothing to fear.

Go and don't look back, I hear her say to me.

I am ready.

I take a stone, a feather, a rose petal, a fishhook.

I must leave behind Troy Jones and the fisherman's wife and even little Onion. I have to go alone.

Troy doesn't understand. *I'm going, too,* he insists.

One of us has to return to the village. If I don't make it back, that someone is you.

Troy is about to argue, but the fisherman's wife makes him understand.

Sometimes it takes as much courage to stay behind as it does to go, she tells him.

It's then he realizes that although he has found our way here, it is my place to go onward.

I move forward, into the darkness.

I am Green, used to being alone in the garden. Green, who can make anything grow. I hasten through the reeds and the tall grass as if I were invisible. Just Green, nothing more. The reeds are my armor and my protection. They are my story, the chapters that have been written and those that have yet to be. My feet are bare and I can feel everything growing right up through me, straight into my heart. I need to be hidden. To be one with the earth. I try to become the meadow I'm walking through. I breathe and think like a meadow. I am silent and still like a meadow.

Yet I move forward.

The Horde must think I'm a weed, a vine, nothing worth paying attention to. Then they hear something in the grass. Me. They turn with their rifles.

My heart is pounding inside my chest. I still have a heart, it seems.

I reach into my pocket for the feather the woman who had lost her children gave me. I hold it up, then let go. The wind carries it past the soldiers. They laugh when they spy the feather, relieved. They believe a bird is hiding in the reeds. That and nothing more. But it's me, Green. Green, who has been in the highest tower, who has slept in the clouds, who has seen doves that can find their way even when they can no longer see, who once heard a lullaby that helped even the most frightened children fall asleep.

Even though I feel I am close to Diamond, I'm afraid that once I find him, one of us will have changed too much for the other to recognize. I will myself to remember what we meant to each other. It all comes back to me. That is what the future is. I see that now. The past and the present entwined into one.

There in the meadow I am no longer so alone, as I'd imagined I would be. I think of my mother, who was always so kind to strangers. She left food out at the end of our road for any passing traveler who might be hungry. She did not judge or place herself above anyone else in this world. You could tell her anything and she would listen. When she worked in the kitchen, boiling quince and apples for jam, rolling out pie crust, shelling beans, every move she made was beautiful. In her hands quince and apples became emeralds, rubies, a treasure. She never used recipes. She made it all up, working by instinct. She had her own ways of doing everything. If she were with me now, she'd tell me to trust myself.

Here is the way, I hear her say to me, and when I go on, I find the prison door.

I use the fishhook the fisherman's wife gave me as a key. It works perfectly. One click and I'm in.

It's murky in the corridors. There's no light inside. I find my way to a staircase that leads to the very top of the tower, where I'd seen the blue flag in the window. It's dark, but I hear the murmur of voices. There are no guards posted inside. Only the soldiers out in the grass. Everyone else is getting ready for the battle. But still, the voices continue.

My eyes adjust to the dark. I see people in cages.

I open the lock of each cage with the fishhook key as I pass by. Some of the people are ours, some are theirs, anyone who has disagreed with their methods or spoken out against violence and hate. Anyone who isn't afraid of the future.

It doesn't matter. In our escape we are brothers and sisters. They are all so grateful they want to follow me, offer their help, but I need to go on alone. I whisper where to find the boat.

Run, I tell them. *Don't be afraid. Don't look back.*

A single night isn't long enough for all I have yet to do. I hurry until I am out of breath.

Once more I'm not as alone as I had believed I would be. I think of my father and how hard he worked. Our garden was nothing but brambles at first. He labored all day long and halfway through the nights, chopping back the tangled weeds, turning the soil, carting away stones, building the fences, the arbors, the well, where the water was always so clear and sweet. He told us we were beautiful, whether or not we were. We could have brambles in our hair, mud on our feet, and it wouldn't matter. He told us we didn't have to do anything to please him, except to be ourselves. Once I saw him crying over a deer a hunter had shot and left to die. I was stunned to see my strong father cry. But now if he were here, he would tell me that real strength has no boundaries.

The more you feel, the stronger you are, I hear him say to me.

Heart, soul, treasure, rain, sister, memory, knowledge, hope, will.

I hurry on, two steps at a time.

I am farther than I've ever been from my garden, yet I still feel the garden inside me. Red roses, sweet peas, blackberries, thorns. Lettuce, squash blossom, verbena, rowan, oak. Each plant that grows there has been a gift to me. Each one has made me stronger.

I remember everything about love as I climb the stairs. It's coming back to me now.

How much does love weigh?

As much as a stone, a feather, a rose petal, a leaf.

It's more than we can ever bear and less than

we have the strength to carry. It is invisible. It's right there in front of me. It's made out of stones. It's made out of air.

At last I come to a cell that is so dark, so hidden, the people inside can't see me. When I whisper a greeting, they don't respond. Thinking I'm one of the guards, they back away. I take the single petal given to me by the red-haired woman who still believes in love. I slip it into the cell. As soon as I do, it turns from white to red. Red as my roses, my blood, my heart.

That's when I see his face in the dark, behind the iron bars.

I open the lock with the fishhook. The metal is light in my hands. Once the prisoners are released, they thank me. Though I don't know their language, I know they are offering me a blessing. I nod, but I see only one person among them.

Diamond.

The other prisoners run down the stairs when I direct them to the boat, but he stays where he is.

Diamond.

He's theirs, but he's mine, too. More mine than anything has ever been.

There is no time for anything, but he kisses me.

I sent you a message, he says.

It is the first time I have heard his voice.

This feels like the greatest blessing of all.

His voice has returned. His throat has healed and he's spent his time in prison learning our language.

This is a gift that is meant for me. He tells me that every time he learned a word, it was to say to me.

I admit that it had taken a very long time to get his message, the painting he'd sent to me, but at last I'd received it. Now I understand that the only thing that had kept us apart were my doubts.

He has been with me even though I haven't been beside him. He tells me so and I believe him.

He says he was captured while searching for his family, thrown onto a black horse, taken here. It was here that he found his family: his mother, his sisters, his cousins. All were in prison with him. Now I've freed them and they are with the group hastening toward the boat.

Now we are together at last.

Before he'd left, I had tattooed his skin. Half a rose, half a thorn, half a wing, half a leaf, half a heart. Diamond found ink and pins in prison and completed each one. He added grass and leaves to the ink he used.

As green as apples, he whispers to me. *As green as the love of my life.*

We climb the highest steps of the tower together. There are two guards there, but Diamond surprises them and locks them in an empty cell. Once they are no longer a threat, he whispers that he knows where Heather is. She's had a child, and lately she's been ill. The father of her child was one of the Horde who was supposed to be her guard but who had fallen in love with her. They'd married in a secret ceremony, attended by prisoners from both sides. But when her husband tried to rescue her, he'd been shot by his own people.

Heather's cell has three locks. They must consider her dangerous. They don't want anyone to see what they've done to her, how much they've taken away. Perhaps even they couldn't find a way to explain a reason for such suffering.

The first lock on her cell is gold, the second is silver, the third is made of iron. They're so strong the fishhook key doesn't work. But I still have the stone taken from my neighbor's field in my pocket, the one that was supposed to tell my future, with a leaf growing inside. I crack off the gold lock and then the silver one. My hands are bleeding by now. Diamond wants to help me, but I know this is something I must do alone.

I come to the last lock, the most difficult one to break. When I hit it, the stone from my neighbor's field crumbles into pieces. All that's left is a single green leaf.

But the lock made of iron has opened. We push in the door.

Heather is holding her baby. It's a boy. A scrawny, weak-looking thing. But his eyes are on me, watching.

Heather, I say. I run to be near her.

She's happy to see me but nearly too exhausted to talk.

I didn't give him a name, she whispers. She and the baby are burning with fever. They stare at something in the distance, as if they can only see some far-off place. *I don't know if he'll last long enough to need a name in this world.*

He'll have a wonderful name, I say. *But now we have to hurry. Your brother sent me. He's waiting for you.*

We run down the flights of stairs. Quick and quiet. There are mice, but we pay no attention. There are bats, but they cling to the rafters, wings folded up tight. The stone steps are cold and stained with blood. We don't want to think about that now. The past is over and done. We're running someplace brand-new.

Down from the tower, down from the cells, out the door, into the grass. There is a dark sky tonight. There are a thousand stars up above. We see the Horde and their stockpiles of gunpowder. We see our village on the other side of the river. It looks as though fireflies have flown into the houses. The generators are working. There are lanterns, candles, flickering lights. The world is returning on the other side. Little by little. Bit by bit. Tonight the river is beautiful. Stars reflect in the black water as if they are a thousand boats that have set sail.

We have to hurry, I tell Heather.

Diamond leads us through the tall grass. We're so close to the gathering of the Horde we can feel the ground shake beneath us. We can hear their raised voices. They have spied our boat and now race to bring cannons out from the storehouse. One cannon is quickly set up in the field and positioned toward the river. If fired, it will go right through our sails, our ship, our lives.

Heather pushes her baby into my arms. When he gazes up at me, I see that his eyes are green. He isn't as scrawny as he first appeared.

If anything happens to me, give him a name, Heather tells me.

I couldn't do that, I sputter. Who am I to do so? Only Green. Not an aunt or a sister or even a cousin.

Of course you can. I think Heather smiles. It's difficult to tell in the dark, but I feel her warmth when she embraces me. *That's what a godmother does*, she says.

Everything happens at once. Heather disappears into the meadow before we can stop her. The Horde has left to bring out the rest of the cannons. As we clamber into the boat, we see that Heather is pushing at the cannon in the field, turning it around.

She is much stronger than a sick, feverish woman should be. She's stronger than she looks.

Some people would no sooner put themselves first than a hawk would choose to stay on the ground, or a dog would refuse to run, or a sparrow would decide to make its home in a cage rather than in the open sky. That's not Heather. She thinks only of us.

She lights the fuse of the cannon. She has turned it toward the storehouse where the weapons are kept. The Horde began this battle. Now the death they wished to offer us is aimed right at them.

Some people understand the will to love

someone. They're not about to give up easily. Heather runs back to us as fast as she can. People watching from the boat later say she was flying. Most believed she would never make it, flying or not. The boat is already leaving the shore, the water is between us, the waves, the black water. Still, Diamond and Troy reach out. They grab her and manage to pull her on board.

When the cannon goes off, there is a moment of quiet. Then the storehouse of gunpowder and weapons is hit. There is a roar as everything on the island disappears in an instant. The tower, the cells, the skulls, the blue flag, the heartache, the Horde.

All of it, up in flames.

The people who destroyed our city have been destroyed by their own weapons.

We close our eyes so they won't fill with ashes. We say a blessing, thankful that we are still alive. Some of us speak one language, some speak another. But that doesn't matter anymore.

I sit with Diamond in the dark as we cross the river. He shows me that he finished the heart tattoo I'd begun on his chest.

It is then I can feel something burn inside me.

Without needles, without pins, without any ink at all, my heart is completed now, too, the color of a rose.

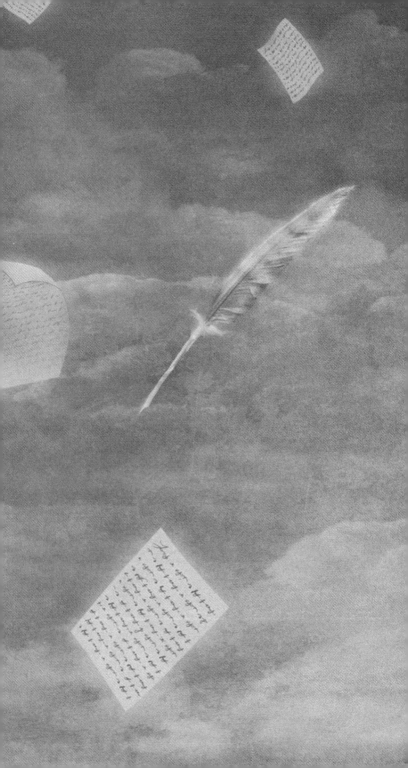

Green Witch

Someone promised me that we all have our own path and that mine could be found in the garden. She said I was the one who was needed most of all.

It was my mother who said that, but I turned away. I didn't believe a word she said. I thought my garden was the last place that would bring me happiness. I thought I was invisible, on my own, meant to be an outsider. Green, who had no life. Green, with no future.

I had no idea that anyone would ever need me.

Now I understand that my mother was right. Once I'd feared that when I finally wrote about the day my family left for the city, it would be the end of the story, the very last page. But that isn't the way it's turned out. My life is opening like a book. It's growing like a garden without any boundaries.

Heather and Troy and the baby moved into our cottage deep in the woods. There are rooms that hadn't been used for so long the doors had to be pried open. It was a pleasure to clean the windows, to wash the sheets and hang them in the sun, to sweep the floors, to make pies and let them cool on the table, to light candles at dinnertime.

We were all so busy I didn't even notice I had turned seventeen.

All through the summer, my neighbor who lived in the stone field brought Heather nettle soup to help bring back her strength. In autumn, the woman who had lost her children brought a cradle and a high chair. That winter, the red-haired woman who still believed in love came to tell stories and Uncle Tim came with her, bringing a toy dog he made out of acorns and reeds. The next spring, the fisherman's wife who had always sewn fishing nets brought a dozen blankets and hats she had knitted.

Every single one was green.

As it turned out I had a gift for Heather as well. I named her baby. I called him Leaf because he had grown from the love all around him. Leaf, because he liked nothing more than to play in the garden. Leaf, with his green eyes and his quiet disposition. Leaf, who was his mother's heart's desire.

All through the year, as we've worked in the garden together and set right the house, I've often said to Heather, *Aren't you lucky I was sent to find you?*

She always laughs out loud.

I am lucky, she agrees. *But he was the one you were meant to find.*

She means Diamond, and she's right about that. I cannot have enough of him. I love the half of his face that is beautiful and the half that was burned in the fire. Most of all I love the part I can't see. The part deep inside. The boy who learned my language, gave me my heart, never left me even when he was so far away.

Diamond's people have moved into villages up and down the river. They are quiet people, brutalized by the same army that brutalized us. Some of them have moved into the city. They have opened shops, markets, concert halls. We listen to their music. We use their recipes, just as they use ours. Our children are in schools together. Our brothers have fallen in love with their sisters, and theirs with ours. We now speak a language that is half and half. The word for *husband* is ours. The word for *wife* is much more beautiful in their dialect. *Adoreé.* We don't seem very different from one another. We have all lost people we love.

On my eighteenth birthday we decide it's time for a party. Two years have passed since the disaster. Two years since I hid under my bed, refusing to face daylight, no longer believing in anything.

Diamond's family crosses the bridge from the city to come to the celebration. His mother has long black hair like mine. She's shy, but wise and proud of her children. She brings along little treasures for the occasion: strong coffee, apple tarts, sesame candies.

Everyone from town has come to celebrate with us. Onion barks at each and every one. The shopkeeper and his wife. My old teacher, the one who remembers every book she's ever read, brings the orphans, dressed in their best clothes. Uncle Tim and the red-haired woman and the white greyhound come up the road together. The fisherman's wife has fixed a stew. The woman who lost her children sings a birthday song. My dear neighbor from the stony field has brought a green nettle cake that is so tall four strong men have to carry it through the field. When it's set on the picnic table outside, the table teeters under its weight. Everyone who eats a piece of my neighbor's cake cries, moved by the sheer emotion of such a fortunate day. We all look at one another and laugh, then toast each other's good health.

Troy Jones has hung strands of white lights all along the fence. He gives some of the orphaned boys the job of turning the hand-cranked generators. Diamond's mother applauds when she sees the lights. It's so glorious to see, like fireflies in the garden. She leans over and whispers in a language I'm beginning to understand. She wishes us happiness for the rest of our lives.

Diamond gives me the best gift of all. A strand of pearls. They are the pearls my mother had planned to present on my sixteenth birthday, the ones I gave to the shopkeeper's wife in exchange for seeds and a warm jacket for Diamond before he went away. He's traded a season's worth of blueberries and two of his paintings to get them back, but the steep price is more than worth it.

Leaf is in the center of everything, there in his carriage. I notice there are vines growing around the wheels, unfolding by the minute. Little seedlings pop up around him. The lilacs bend in his direction, drawn to him. He is my godchild, so I'm not surprised. I am the Green Witch, after all, the one who can bring your heart's desire. In time I'll teach Leaf everything I learned from my mother. How to bury old boots beside pear trees so they will bear the sweetest fruit. How to spray roses with garlic so aphids will go elsewhere. Before long, Leaf will only have to whisper and the wisteria will bloom. He'll laugh and the tomatoes will ripen overnight.

But I will have to come back to teach him these lessons. Diamond and I are leaving for the city. The world that was so ruined is growing brighter. It shines like silver at night, gold in the sun. The city was always my garden, the people there like flowers, the traffic like a river, the lights of the buildings shining as if they were a hundred white tears. Our stand will be set up in the square where my family was selling vegetables on that day. We have already chosen the space. Troy and Heather and Leaf will bring us lettuce and string beans and baskets of pears. They will tell us stories about the village and we will show them all that's brand-new in the city. At night we will sit at one of the cafés, my sister's little dog, Onion, beside us. We will know how lucky we are.

I am the last person anyone would have expected to believe in the future, but I do. I am not hurrying toward it anymore. I am inside of it. A lifetime, after all, can be spent in a single afternoon. A world can exist in a kiss, a rose, a leaf, a heart. On my window ledge I will always keep three stones: silver for my mother, black for my father, white as the moon for my sister, Aurora.

Late at night, when the marketplace is quiet, when the boy I have always loved is asleep, I will sit in my kitchen with my typewriter. The city is not what it once was — buildings have fallen, parks have burned, trains still don't run. All the same, it's filled with stories, far too many to count. Too many to ever write down in a single lifetime.

Some people say there's nothing but piles of bricks here. They say we'll never be able to build our city again. They say our gardens are gone, but they're wrong.

There are already roses growing outside my door.

Acknowledgments

With gratitude to my brilliant editor, David Levithan, who knew exactly how Green's story should be told; to the amazing Elizabeth Parisi, art director and magician who created Green's world; and to the extraordinary artist, Matt Mahurin, who brought Green to life.

To my readers, thank you for telling me the story wasn't over.